BUSTER GETS BRACES

BUSTER GETS BRACES

STORY AND PICTURES BY
JANE BRESKIN ZALBEN

HENRY HOLT AND COMPANY   NEW YORK

Published by Henry Holt and Company, Inc., 115 West 18th Street, New York, New York 10011.
Published simultaneously in Canada by Fitzhenry & Whiteside Ltd., 91 Granton Drive, Richmond Hill, Ontario L4B 2N5.

Library of Congress Cataloging-in-Publication Data
Zalben, Jane Breskin.   Buster gets braces / story and pictures by Jane Breskin Zalben.
Summary: After being fitted with braces, Buster copes with having to eat mushy foods and hearing his sister's teasing.
[1. Orthodontics—Fiction.   2. Brothers and sisters—Fiction.]   I. Title.
ISBN 0-8050-1682-1   PZ7.Z254Bu   1991   [E]—dc20   91-13967

Printed in the United States of America on acid-free paper. ∞
Typography by Jane Breskin Zalben
3   5   7   9   10   8   6   4   2

The art was done with a 000 brush using watercolors,
and Prismacolored pencils on imported Italian paper.
The display type is Busorama. The interior text is Optima.

TO ALEXANDER,
MY BIRTHDAY BOY WITH BRACES,
WHO INSPIRED ME

Weeks before my older brother Buster's birthday party, Dr. Orville told our parents, "Buster needs braces." "Too bad," I said to Buster, trying to look extra sad. "Cross off those tacos for lunch." Buster covered his mouth, stared at the plaster molds of teeth lining the shelves, and mumbled, "Why me?"

As Mom and Dad drove past Stanley's Rib Joint,
Buster moaned, "In a few weeks, no more bones."
"Speak for yourself, kemo sabe," I teased.

That night at dinner, Buster was miserable, nursing each kernel of corn on the cob as though it were the last one he'd be having for his entire life. Until his return visit to Dr. Orville's office, Mom cooked all his favorite meals. So did Dad. "Gee," I reminded Buster, as I chomped down on hard French bread, "you won't be able to chew through applesauce when you get braces." Buster opened his mouth full of food. "Yuck!" I cried.

After his braces were put on, Dr. Orville gave
him stickers that said "I Love My Orthodontist!"
She told Buster to gargle with salt water. And he did.
To the tune of "Take Me Out to the Ball Game."
"Sounding good," I shouted outside the bathroom
door as I recorded it.

I played the song for everyone in the playground.
Buster called me "Sally, the pain in the valley."
I called him "Metal Mouth." Everyone laughed.
I brought thick peanut-butter-and-jelly sandwiches
for lunch while he ate soggy tuna fish. I pointed
at the shredded bits of celery stuck in his braces.
And I yelled, "Lizard Thing, you make my heart sing!"
Some of the rubber bands on his teeth shot out into
Thelma Goldberg's yogurt. "Worms!" she screamed.

On the school bus, I blew large pink bubbles.
He exploded the gum on my face.

"I'm telling," I cried.
"Tell," said Buster. "See if I care."

As the day of Buster's birthday party got closer,
he made a list of friends. "I'm scratching
out your name, Pest Breath," he said to me.
"And no one can make me invite you," he added.

My mother made him put my name back on.
Everything he wanted to have at his party was
off limits. "My life is the pits!"
Buster groaned, growing sadder and sadder.

At twelve o'clock, on October 29, the doorbell rang.
Buster opened the front door. His three best friends,
Marty, Thelma, and Terry, smiled. So did Buster.
Shining silver covered their canines.

"Metal never looked so good," my mother
whispered to my father while he made lunch.
"Pasta for everyone!" Dad shouted.
It slid down their throats with no chewing.

Buster unwrapped his birthday presents.
Thelma got him a gift certificate at Gerald's Jelly Beans,
good for five years, and a year's supply of toothpaste.
Marty brought a three-way mirror, so Buster could see
his mouth from every angle, and a new red toothbrush.

Terry made him a member of their club with a secret recipe for the best peanut brittle in the whole world. "Where's your gift, Sally sweetheart?" Mom asked. She had taken me to get it last Wednesday after tap dancing. "I forget," I said, knowing I'd left Buster's present at the bottom of my pajama drawer. Buster rolled his eyes.

When Mom brought out the cake, the light from the candles

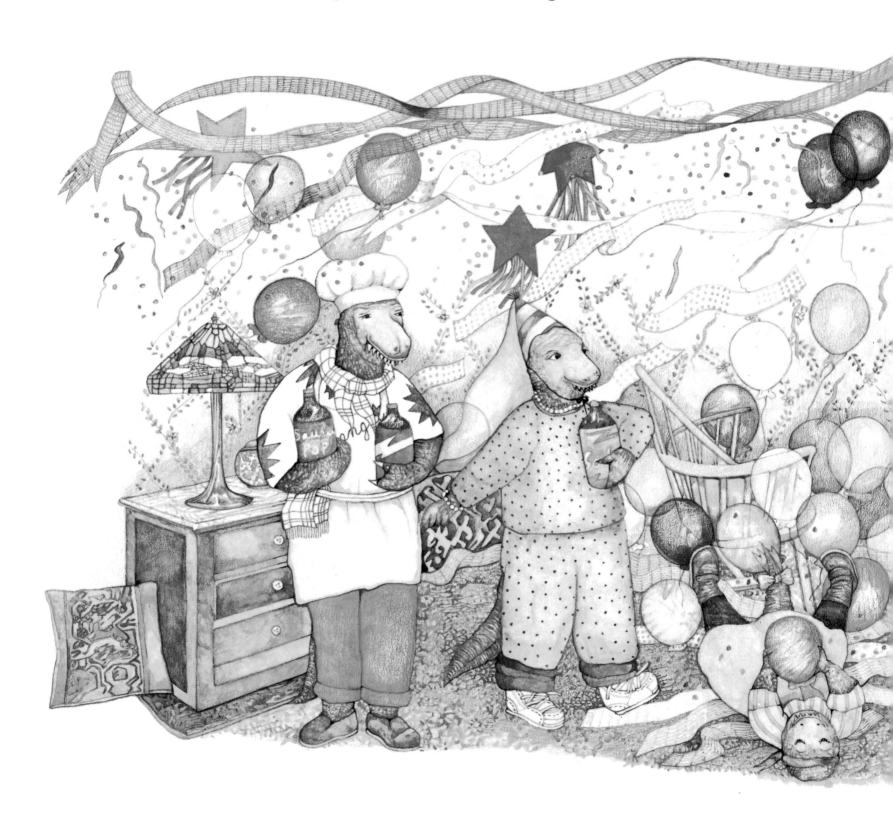

glowed on Buster's braces while we sang "Happy Birthday."

The next morning, I woke up with a toothache.
Mom said, "Buster darling, would you walk Sally
next door? I'll be there in a few minutes."

Buster smiled the largest smile I had ever seen when he heard the dentist say, "Cavities! No more sweets! Soft foods tonight." Now I knew how Buster felt.

We both ate mush for dinner.
"Poor Sally," Mom said.
"Poor Buster," Dad said.

"Here's your present," I said while we brushed our teeth.
Buster opened a large envelope. Inside was an IOU
for two dozen spareribs at Stanley's. Good for any time.
And a card that said in large letters "I'M SORRY!"
Buster gave me a nooggie on the head. "Truce?" he asked.
I gave him a punch back. "Truce," I said.

But when I got into my room, Buster was waiting for me. With a bucket of buttered popcorn.